I0636380

BEFORE MY TIME

FLAMES OF POETRY

BEFORE MY TIME

Flames of Poetry

By Crystal Gonzales Michel

Print book ISBN:979-8-218-45803-4

Introduction

Born July of 1980 in a small town of about 21,000 during that time. Madera California is where I was born, and grew up my entire life. Before My Time Flames of Poetry, came about shortly after October 4th 2023, after getting news from a Neurologist that I had been seeing for sometime, explained that there was some abnormal findings in the brain, that my memory will be affected as well as my ability to think, read and write amongst other things that will lead to my demise. My heart was crushed to say the least. To imagine not being able to do the things I love to do has caused my heart to ache deep into my core. But with that news, it also allowed me to put my pin to paper. I came from a broken home. Alcoholic parents, an abusive father, a battered mother. Reading and writing was an escape, to drown out the noise in my mind. Writing for me came naturally early on as a child. Music reading and writing was a coping mechanism I used throughout my entire life. It got me through the struggles of living in unsafe environments. I was able to write all that I was feeling good and bad, and transformed it into something beautiful. It was also a way to express my heartache and pain into existence. I didn't know how to control all my emotions so writing became an outlet. Growing up in a broken home, I knew struggle very well. There's no doubt that I had to grow up with tough skin. But, today I struggle with knowing that losing my ability to think, read, write will affect every part of my livelihood. In an effort to leave an imprint for my children before my time, that all things are possible. To never doubt your ability to do something great, no matter what that may be. The gift of your imagination is great. Even if no one else believes, I believe in you. To my beautiful five, you are all perfect to me, so I leave you with this, words that will last a lifetime. You have given me everything one's heart can desire.

If I can give you anything before my time on this earth is over,

it's to see yourselves through my eyes, I love you forever.

Dedication

We often think we have more time in life than we actually do. Never should we take for granted those we hold dear. We fail to tell those we love assuming we'll always have time. The truth is, in this life, it's all just a means to an end, it's inevitable. So take chances, love fiercely. We only get one chance at life, make it a good one.

Throughout our lives we are pulled in so many different directions that we lose sight of the important things. Being a mom at 14 is undoubtedly challenging. Your whole life changes. We are now responsible for a little person, and it's no longer about you, it's about the little life you just brought into this world. There wasn't a question if you were ready, you have to be.

I hope my children know that though a young mother, they were all that mattered to me in this world. I wouldn't change it even if I could. We learned and grew together, and I know that was hard at times. I hope this book can help give you a little piece of me wherever you go.

I've spent many years writing. I didn't think it was possible to do something with it, let alone publish a book of my own, and share it with the world. We all have what it takes so long as we put our minds to it, for me I put my heart and soul into this.

If I can thank anyone for becoming the person I am today. The credit would have to go to my oldest brother Ruben. You never gave up on me. I know you did the best you could raising my brother and I under the circumstances, I will be forever grateful.

To those that I may have crossed paths with throughout my life you in some way gave my life meaning.

And to my beautiful five my love for you is infinite

I hope that for all my readers you can connect with this book deeply ,as I have written it.

Contents

Seasons

The years go by as seasons change,

From springtime and summer, winter and rain.

Our bodies and mind, are as such,

From happiness and laughter,

To heartache and pain.

And in that moment, I start to see,

The weight of the world consumes me.

No matter the season, weather sunshine or rain,

I'll walk beside you forever,

For our hearts are intertwined,

They'll forever beat the same.

The Darkness

I'm not afraid of the darkness,

That lives inside me.

For it carries me through the fire,

That ignites deep within me.

And if somehow, I see the light,

I'm afraid to see what will become of me.

Will it tear me down, or set me free.

I'm not afraid of the darkness,

For it comforts me,

For it carries me the the fire, that's ignited

Deep within me.

Music

I listen to the music,

When my thoughts are too loud .

It takes me to another place,

But only for a while.

The weight of my thoughts consume me,

Music…. Come rescue me!!

For , it's the only thing that sets me free.

But only for a moment, does it dull down the pain,

Of the loudness of my thoughts,

Running through my mind.

Music is serenity,

It takes me to another place, but only for a while.

I Am Wrath

I am wrath,

But, you can not see,

The storm that's forming, inside of me.

I pray to God to calm the storm,

And in that moment, a rainbow forms.

I watch the waves,

Of the dangerous sea,

But , it's the sound of the ocean,

That comforts me.

I look past the waves of the dangerous sea,

Because it calms the storm forming inside of me.

I Cried

I cried myself to sleep last night,

And today, I cried, still…

To hear your voice, it soothes my heart,

But, the heartache I still feel.

Twenty four years ago, I birthed you,

But then, you hadn't the slightest clue

How much I truly love you,

And all the things you do.

I know this journey may lead you,

To an unknown, far away place

I only wish to hold you,

With that smile upon your face.

Into The Light

As you walk in darkness,

I feel pain.

The feeling of failure as a mother,

I cry in the rain.

My heart aches deep in my soul,

A brokenness that lingeries down to my core,

I try to remember, that God

Is in control.

I pray to God with all my might,

You'll step out of the darkness.

And into the light.

Where You Are

No matter where you are,

No matter near or far,

My heart will always be exactly,

Where you are.

Although my days feel troubled,

Because we're thousands of miles apart.

Just close your eyes to see,

That i'm exactly where you are.

So never doubt my presence,no matter

near or far,

My heart will always be exactly,

Where you are.

Your Touch

I looked into your eyes, and for a moment,

My world stood still.

The racing of two hearts, that,

Didn't seem quite real.

You pulled me close and kissed my lips,

I was lost in the moment,

When your hands gripped my hips.

My body shaking from your touch,

Scared to want you, oh so much.

But I crave to feel your very touch..

A Moment In Time

When the autumn leaves have fallen,

And the cold sets in.

Don't forget to breathe in the magic,

That my touch left on your skin.

The warmth of your body, as it touches mine,

It takes me to another place,

Another moment in time.

You light a fire, deep in my soul,

As if, you've known me for a lifetime,

You make me feel whole.

Life

Appreciate life, even if it makes you blue,

A broken heart, but a lesson,

You'll always make it through.

There's a greater purpose in life,

One day you will see,

Just dig a little deeper, it's just beneath the surface.

So appreciate life, even if it makes you blue,

The ache won't last forever,

You'll always make it through.

Fight

Despite your attempts to live your life right,

The demons are quick to put up a fight.

People say, through the darkness,

There's always a light.

But, why can't I see it..

It seems out of sight.

Maybe, this life is out of my hands,

Show me the light, and all its demands.

Only God can show me the way,

And never leave me astray

.

The demons are quick to put up a fight,

Guide me through the darkness, lead me to happiness.

I Vow

I vow to love you, with all my heart.

Through sickness and health,

Whether we're together, or apart.

Love is greater than all else,in this world,

I'll give you my heart,

To have and to hold,

Even through hardship, my heart will love, still.

There's no changing this heart,

And the love that I feel.

If I May Fall

If at some point, I may fall,
It's only for a little while, before I rise,
Above it all..

Life isn't easy, this, I know..
For I've had my struggles, of highs and lows.

I'm not perfect, nor have I tried to be.
And life, but a lesson,
This I can see

.

I struggled to make it all my life,
And thus learned to fight to survive.

People greet you while trying to defeat you.

But if at some point I may fall,

It's only for a while before. I rise,
Above it all.

If Tomorrow Never Comes

If tomorrow never comes my way.

Just know, that, I love you with all my heart,
today..

We are never promised forever,
But, in my heart you'll always stay..

So when it's dark,
And the light, seems too far to see,

Just close your eyes, and think of me,
Because in your heart, I'll always
be..

Hope

Never give up fighting,

Even if you're feeling blue, and the world seems to,

Be crumbling around you.

It takes a lot to change a man, even,

A man like you.

You are no exception,

No one in this life is out of God's reach.

If you open up your mind,

You'll see, he has a lot to teach.

So never give up fighting, even if you're feeling blue

And the world seem to be, crumbling

Around you

.

It takes a lot to change a man,

Even a man like you.

Damien

Set Me Free

Beneath my flesh, I feel emptiness,

And even though I love, I can't reach happiness.

I'm smiling outside, but going insane.

Because beneath the surface,

I feel pain.

And my sunny days have turned to rain

This heart has turned cold,

The chill consumes me

If there's a flicker of light, left in me,

Ignite the darkness, deep within me,

Set me free..

Still Waters

Calming , still waters of the deep

blue sea.

Something in the waters, surrounds

Me.

It makes me surrender,

True tranquility.

I walk along the beach I love,

Where sunshine fills the sky above.

Calming, still waters of the

deep blue sea.

Rescue me..

I'm Losing Me

This ache in my heart is getting harder

to bare,

To know of this life ending,

It cuts deep, through the walls of my core.

Every thought, and emotion in my heart,

Weighs on me.

I feel as if, i'm losing this fight,

The future, so far in the distance,

It's hard to see,

I'm losing,

Me.

When this ache in my heart, is weighing

On me.

Serenity

The rays of the sunlight, cutting beautifully

through the trees,

The weightless touch of the wind, breathing

through me.

The feeling of solid ground,

Beneath my feet.

Beautiful

The sound of the ocean, yet treacherous

beneath the surface.

It carries me through the storm surrounding me

Giving me a sense of peace,

Deep serenity.

Georgia

Georgia, where the fear inside me ends,

And happiness begins.

.

It touches a part of my soul,

A mosaic of tranquility,

Cuts through me.

Setting ablaze, every dark space inside me

Free

Georgia , where the fear ends,

And happiness begins.

A place where my heart feels fulfillment,

Georgia.

Infinite

Everywhere the light touches,

Captures the depths of the darkness inside my soul,

My heart,

infinite , like the ocean waves.

Calm, but treacherous,

A lasting emotion my heart craves.

The ever changing tides,

Of the infinite sea, overpowering me,

Storms, raging through me,

Like the treacherous sea.

This Flame

The weight of this pain,

Will not stop this burning flame

The fire in my soul .

Will never turn to coal.

As long as this fire burns deep

Inside my soul

The weight of this pain,

Will never stop this burning flame,

Not even the winter, and its,

Pouring rain.

Broken Wings

I search for a way, to repair these broken wings,

But, it seems as though,

They Are apart of me, amongst,

Other things.

I feel my soul ache, as my heart bleeds.

A coldness of darkness,

That, nobody sees.

As I search for a way, to move

past this pain.

I'll continue soar endlessly,

With these broken wings.

Before My Time

Before my time on this earth,comes to an end,

I'll hold close,

all the great moments we've shared,

And smile, about all the crazy things we've said.

Every pound of our heart beats were felt,

When you pulled your body close

to mine.

Nothing, can erase the feeling we felt,

Not even the ever moving time.

Walk beside me, once more for just a little while,

So, when my days on earth are done,

You'll think of me and smile.

Regrets

Lying here awake in my bed,

Regretting all the things, I should have said.

Tomorrow I'll wake,

With thoughts of regrets,

Not saying the things, in my heart,

Words I know, I should have said.

And maybe, one day you will see, just how much,

You really meant to me.

Lying here awake alone in my bed,

Regretting all the things I should have said.

Horizon

I crave the beautiful stillness, of

the orange horizon,

It captures the beauty,of earth's surface

and ember skies.

As though, two souls meet.

There's no gravity strong enough

On the surface, to hold me

Still.

It's the beautiful stillness, of the orange

horizon,

My heart craves to feel.

Coal

My soul ignites a fire,

To light up the darkness inside my soul,

My heart still breaking,

From the coal inside my soul.

Torn by the weight that this heart holds.

The weight of my thoughts,

Heavy and loud.

The depths of my soul, ache

An ache, I can't seem to shake, from

This coal inside my soul.

Summer Breeze

Airy, like the night summer breeze,

Cutting through so effortless,

Through the evergreen trees.

The weightless touch of the wind,

Touches every part of my exposed skin.

Airy, like the night summer breeze.

Serenity fills the air, as the weightless breeze,

Blows through every single strand of my

long brown hair.

Our Eyes First Met

When the day comes to an end, and

the sun starts to set,

I'll always remember, the light in your eyes,

When our eyes first met.

And when they met mine, the very first time,

I couldn't help, but feel the fire,

Between your soul and mine.

You take my breath away, in every single way,

The feeling of fulfillment, fills a void,

But, we were never meant to stay.

Fields Of Garden

Fields of garden, I long to see,

The uneven surface beneath my feet.

The depths of the mountains,

Surrounding me.

The orange of the infinite horizon,

True tranquility.

It touches every part of the fire , lit

Inside my soul.

I ache for the moment my heart feels whole,

Fields of garden, comfort me,

Lead me to a place, I long to be free.

Love

Love is a hunger, every heart craves to feel,

A love like pure magic,

That,

For a moment, hold you still.

Life still goes on, with or without it.

But, in your heart,

You're thankful you found it.

Even if, one day, your heart breaks.

Your thankful for the chance to love,

Rather than, live a lifetime without it.

Love for a moment,

Will hold your heart still.

Love is a hunger every heart craves to feel.

The Depths Of Two Hearts

Understanding the connections of two hearts,

And its depths,

It touches your soul, with unspoken words,

In such a way, so gently.

That only your heart understands,

By the way, it makes you feel.

Two hearts burning, in the heat, of

Each Other's arms.

Caressing every curve of your body,

Like the music notes of a song.

The Man In Disguise

There's a house, that once built me,

When I was a child,

A house in the country, with demons

Inside.

From cussing and fighting,

My mothers, desperate cries.

Angry and scared, the night had arrived,

And so did the devil, a man,

In disguise.

There's a house, that once built me,

When I was a child,

A house in the country, with darkness inside.

A house that held secrets, and

the man in disguise.

Finding My Identity

Pushing and pulling, to shake

This insanity,

And find my identity

I don't even know what to do with myself.

Trying to refrain from losing myself.

Awakened by the echoes, inside my head.

Every turn of emotions consumes me.

From the chaos,

As I lie awake in this empty bed.

Pushing and pulling, to rid myself,

From this insanity,

And find my identity.

Every Time Our Eyes Meet

Every time our eyes meet,

Your voice breathes,

The last whisper, before I go to sleep.

When I wake, its walls I see,

I need to share your company.

And

Every once in a while,I get the ache,

To tell you how I feel.

Every time our eyes meet,

Your voice breathes,

The last whisper before I go to sleep.

Hourglass

How long will this ache last,

Holding on to the time,

Where the hourglass meets the past.

When the night falls, and

And the world is quiet.

I lie awake in darkness,

Listening to the whispers of my conscience.

Before I go to sleep,

Holding on tight, to the time,

Where the hourglass meets the past.

Little Girl

From the moment you arrived,

The moment you opened your eyes,

My heart already knew,

I'd spend the rest of my life,

Loving you.

Watching you grow,

Has been my greatest blessing, that

You'll ever know.

There's no one in this world quite like you,

My precious little girl.

Warm Embrace

The day that I held you,

I already knew,

I didn't want to walk, without

The anticipation of walking towards

You.

And I know it makes no sense.

I want to walk in the shadows of your,

Warm embrace.

Desiring to feel the burn,

Your touch left on my skin.

The weight of your hand, upon my face,

Remembering every touch,

Of your warm embrace.

The Simple Things

As I walk this earth, my heart

Craves to see,

The beauty of life, all around me,

And the simple things.

I don't wish for luxuries or material things,

I wish to see, the light of life

In front of me.

As I walk this earth, I ache to fill a void,

That haunts me in my sleep.

My heart craves to see, the magic of

God's creation, the beauty of life,

The simple things.

Willow Tree

Beneath the old willow tree,

Is where my life as a child,

Felt most free.

The breath of the country air, breathing

right through me.

The leaves of the old willow tree,

Blowing effortless,

All around me.

Where my life as a child,

Felt most free.

Take me back to the country,

Beneath that old willow tree.

Scars Of My Heart

The person I am today,

Will never hide the scars, of who

I am inside.

The scars of my heart,

For which they are written,

Won't erase the feeling,

For which my heart is bleeding.

These scars, are a part of me,

I won't keep them hidden.

It's the fire in my soul,

That keeps my heart beating.

The burning flame within me, reminds me

I'm still human.

Guide Me To The Light

The thought of, a glimpse of light,

Burning through me,

Allows my soul to see, hope,

A silver lining.

I hope to see, one day,

The gift of life, within my reach.

And if my life, may,

Escape me,

I pray that God guides me to the light,

That,

Sets my soul free.

Casualties Of War

I tell myself, if I withdrawl, from those who care,

The weight, when i'm gone, won't be,

Quite as heavy.

I create an illusion, inside my mind,

That saves them, from the casualties of war

Inside my head.

The weight of this life, and its uncertainty,

It's burning a hole, right through me.

As I lie awake alone in my bed,

The chaos of my thoughts, roaming through my head,

With words unsaid.

I create this illusion in my head, that

Saves them from the casualties of war inside my head.

Secrets Inside

We live in a world, of make believe,

Where a house full of secrets

lie inside.

Hiding the demons, who

Live there inside.

The man in the shadows, with

Darkness in his eyes.

Darkness awaits inside, in hide.

He lived in a world of make believe.

Where a house full of secrets

Lie inside

Trying to hide from the demons,

Who resides there inside.

Through The Fire

I didn't walk through the fire,

To see them , watch the flame,

Nor did I

Walk through the depths of fire,

To watch me burn, in pain.

The fire that, resides deep within me,

Is the flame that drives me.

I'll never try to hide

The girl with fire in her eyes

That lives inside me.

You And Me

Meet me at the endless beauty,

On the horizon.

Where the embers meet the sea.

Take me to a place of beauty.

Where there's just,

You and me.

Kiss me until, the dark,

Meets the sunrise in the morning.

Meet me at the beautiful

Horizon,

Where the embers meet the sea,

Where there's just,

You and me.

Meet Me At The Ocean

If ever, you want to feel me near,

I'll never be far away.

Meet me at the ocean, where the

salt water meets the sand.

It is there, that you will find me,

If you want to hold my hand.

Though I know,

The days go by, as seasons change, but

You never are alone.

So if ever you want to feel me near,

I'll never be far away.

It is there that, you will find me,

If you want to hold my hand.

Meet me at the ocean, where the

salt water meets the sand.

Embers Of My Soul

There's a mosaic of beauty,

In the waves of the sea.

Touching every grain of sand, of

the land's simplicity.

The ever moving strength ,of the

tidal waves, move me..

As does the iceberg's transparency.

The bright orange everglow,

The embers of my soul,

Will light up the depths, of the darkness

Oceans floor.

Poetry In My Veins

I have a ache for you, in my heart, and

poetry in my veins.

For that, my love for you,

Will never cease to change.

Even as I walk through the darkness,

In a winter haze,

The way your eyes met mine,

Longing with gaze.

Your poetry on my lips,

For that, my love for you,

Will never cease to change.

For I, have poetry of you, running through

My veins.

A Little While

If ever, there comes a time,

We have to say goodbye.

I'll think of you, always, and the way

You made me feel.

If having you for a little while,

Is all the time we had,

Id rather had held you, a little while

Than,

Never had held you at all.

Weight Of My Thoughts

The heavy weight of my thoughts,

Play out, a hundred times

in my head.

As the world around me, quiets,

My mind lies awake.

I lie awake in darkness, in wait,

Just for the sun to rise.

The weight of mt thoughts, scrambling

with chaos.

Aching for an ounce of peace,

To put my mind at rest.

Remember You

I'll remember you, for a lifetime,

Cause I know,

You too, feel the same.

And there's nothing about,

You and I,

That, my heart would ever change.

You created memories in my heart,

That, my mind can't erase.

You drew me in,

Like a moth drawn to a flame.

A feeling so strong we couldn't explain.

I'll remember you, for a lifetime,

And, that will never change.

Painted Pictures

You painted pictures in my heart,

That, my mind can't erase.

Your the ghost, that lives within,

The walls of my heart.

Haunted by the thoughts, and

memories of you and me,

Within

Thoughts of what could have been..

And it's easy to see,

You painted pictures in my heart,

Of you and me.

Heavens Gates

If I never see the promise,

On this side of heaven's gates.

Walk with me,

Until my journey,

Meet the other side of my fate.

I'll walk this earth,

Through your infinite light,

Where my destiny awaits.

Where, I hope to see the promise,

At the end of heaven's gates.

Think Of Me And Smile

If the time comes,

And I must say, goodbye,

Remember that, Gods plan,

Is greater than, your and mine.

And if ever, you find yourself thinking

of me,

I hope you think of me and smile.

And

Remember that, God's plan,

Is greater than your and mine.

Melodies And Symphonies

Dirt roads and willow trees,

Summer nights in the august heat.

Melodies and symphonies,

Sunsets and summer breeze,

Country air, and the simple things.

Takes me back to who I used to be,

Of the country breeze, and memories.

The sail of the wind,

Singing,

Melodies and symphonies.

Rage

There's a war of rage, that

lives inside me.

Destroying everything around,

In its wake.

An ache so cold, it cuts so deep,

Beneath

My skin and bones.

When the ache settles, and the dust clears,

I'll still the depths, of

this growing rage.

This war of rage, inside me,

Treacherous,

Destroying everything around,

In its wake.

Spirits And Demons

These feelings i'm feeling,

Brings me no healing,

From this heartache,

Spirits and demons.

If there's a silver lining ,

Why, Can't reach it!!

It's getting harder to drown out,

The noise,

From the chaos my mind is hearing.

Theses feelings i'm feeling,

Brings me no healing,

Of this heartache,

Spirits and demons.

.

Anguish From Within

If I focus on my purpose,

Rather than my pain.

Will it walk me through the

Darkness,

And out of this, pouring rain.

Darkness is all, I have ever known,

Of the anguish I feel within,

But it's where, I learned to find myself,

Underneath,

These layers of skin.

Survive

Everyday of my life, i've fought to stay alive,

An alcoholic father, an unstable mother.

Running in the cold,

From one place to another.

I've learned to be fearless,

Everyday of my life,

And push the tears, deep down,

All the silent cries.

Running and fighting,

Just to survive.

But, God, was walking with me,

The fight was never mine..

Flames Of Poetry

The flames of poetry,

Breathing life,

Through the walls of my heart.

The flames of fire, burn deep

It resides deep inside, my soul and mind.

Awakening the mystery,

Of who I am inside.

Ignited by the fire of this wild heart of mine.

Touched by the flames of poetry.

It's the only thing that gives me the will,

To survive,

The mystery that awakens me,

The flames of poetry.

The Fire

I have a fire burning, deep in my core,

It echoes throughout,

The depths of my soul.

A fire so bright, it lights up the night.

Burning everything around,

In its sight.

The wrath of my rage,

Ignited by fire.

Burning through everything around,

In its sight.

Tides Of The Ocean

The highest tides of the ocean,

Surround me.

There's no calming, these raging

tidal waves inside me.

As treacherous as it seems, to be

It's every bit a part of me.

The weight of my soul cold,as the depths

On the ocean floor.

But, as treacherous as it may seem,

It's every bit a part of me.

Clouds Of Gray

Clouds of gray are moving,

Across the infinite sky,.

You'll never know, afar, that I weep for you

And cry.

And if by chance, our paths may cross.

Once more,

In this life or the next.

Remember how, you felt for me,

And the imprint your heart left on mine.

Though,

Clouds of gray are moving,

Across the infinite sky.

Don't forget to think of me,

And how you made me smile.

Already Home

Starting to feel the anxiety, of leaving

this beautiful place.

A place of pure comfort, that

only my heart knows..

A place that makes me forget,

All my highs and lows.

And perhaps, it's the answer,

My heart already knows.

My heart has already,

Made this beautiful place my home.

Lightning Strike

Have you ever, looked at someone,

So deep into their eyes.

And knew,

That in some way,

They came to change your life,

Although,

Lightning never strikes, the same place twice.

When our eyes met, yet again,

I knew that in some way,

You came to change my life.

Lightning struck, the same place twice,

Between,

Your heart and mine.

Magic In Your Eyes

There's magic in the sunset,

Only my eyes can see.

Touching every part of my soul,

Like the surface, of the oceans

Beautiful infinite sea.

The rays of the sunlight,

Cutting beautifully through the trees.

I see it in the stars, I see it in your

Eyes.

A light that lights the darkness,

The embers of magic, in your eyes.

Echoes Of The Wind

The orange everglow, over the horizon,

Melts the gray skies away.

All my wounds and my mistakes,

Begin to fade away.

The echoes of the wind, breathing,

Fearlessly

Beneath the great big sky.

Whispers of melodies, singing

Effortlessly

And all my wounds and my mistakes,

Begin to fade away.

Raging Storm

If I look past the storm, and out of the rain,

Will it take away,

All this heartache and pain.

And if i'm being honest,

There's a raging storm , running through

My veins.

Nothing can stop it,

It seems to know me by name.

I'm reckless by nature,

That will never change.

For there a raging storm, running through

My veins.

Darkness Knows Me

I know the darkness well,

And the darkness knows me.

I may have a wild soul,

But, I'm a lover of simple things.

Though,

I may never see the light,

Lay with me in the darkness,

Let me be me,

Let my mind run free.

For I know the darkness well,

And the darkness knows me.

Better Off Apart

You and I promised , that

We would never part.

But, if loving you, is fighting demons,

We're better off apart.

The cost of loving you,

It is a tragedy in the heart.

Were holding on to a love,

Otherwise gone from sight.

And if loving you, is fighting demons

We're better off apart.

Foolish

It was foolish of me,

To dive right in,

To the thought of you and me.

What remains, of you and me,

Is just another, distant memory.

But I can't help, but think of you,

And how things used to be.

The memories that we created, when

You were close to me.

Fire Unites Us

I'll walk through the flame,

And rise from the ashes.

Where the fire connects us,

And somehow, unites us.

So let it be me,

Whom you crave to see.

Though,

Hell on the heart,

That's what reminds us.

It's the flame, that

Ignites us,

And somehow unites us.

Beside You

I walked this earth, beside you,

Through the thunder, and the rain.

In hopes, that

You'll see someday,

The heartache, and the pain.

But, the more I stood beside you,

The more things stayed the same.

And maybe I ignored the signs,

That things would never change.

Whisper Of Your Kiss

And every whisper of your kiss,

Was dangerous and amiss.

But, how I long to feel your energy,

That your kiss,

Left upon my lips.

An ache, I seem to know so well,

It lingeries,

To the very core of my soul.

And every whisper of your kiss,

Was dangerous and amiss.

Out Of The Blue

You came into my life,

Out of the blue.

You made a lasting impression,

This much is true.

And no matter the distance,

Or what you may, say or do,

Your stuck on my heart,

I'll never live this life,

Without thinking of you.

You made a lasting impression,

This much is true.

In The Still Of The Night

Sit with me awhile,

In the still of the night.

Hold me tight, while I cry,

And fall apart.

Just, until I feel alright.

Kiss me slow, and hold me tight,

Till my eyes meet the sunrise,

Morning light.

Sit with me awhile,

In the still of the night.

Ultimate Sin

Every touch of your hand,

As it caresses my skin.

The taste of your kiss, upon my lips,

The ultimate sin.

Thoughts of you, within

Before my day begins.

Lingering throughout,

Every part of my body, within

You're stuck in my heart, I won't forget.

Consumed by every emotion,

Of you herein.

An ache for your touch,

The ultimate sin.

Shadows

Standing in the shadows,

of my old self.

Picking up the pieces, that

Broke when I fell.

The nightmares, consuming me, from

The chaos of eternal hell.

Shadows of my old self,

Stand beside me.

Hoping to piece together, my life,

And the part of me,

That broke when I fell.

Have You Ever

Have you ever loved someone,

So much,

Even though they broke your heart.

You promised them forever,

though , toxic from the start.

Heaven knows,

I've tried to love, without fault.

But, it's only causing chaos, within

From the one who broke my heart.

Lead Me

Lead me to the rock,

Higher than you and I.

Where I can see the light,

Before I fall apart.

Illuminate the darkness,

Where the demons hide inside

My mind.

Lead me to the highest of mountains,

Higher than you and I,

Where I can see the light.

At Bay

You will never understand,

The depths of my flaming soul.

So I always, keep my distance,

And never, get too close.

Keeping my heart guarded,

With a double edged sword,

These feelings of mine, so passionate,

I keep at bay,

So you will never know.

That, the ache won't be so great,

The day I let you go.

Who I Am Inside

My feeling for you, I can't hide,

Although you mean a lot to me,

I can't let you see,

The darkness I carry inside.

For I don't think you would,

Understand,

All the nights I lay awake and cried.

I just keep these feelings

Hidden.

So you won't know,

Who I am inside.

Lost At Sea

When the weight of the ache,

Is too heavy,

And I can't seem to see,

I'll sit in darkness,

Until, the light awakens me.

My thoughts, lost at sea.

Perhaps it's the answer to finding

Me.

Lost in the trenches, of the unforgiving

Sea

Where the undertow, seeks the land,

Where the water meets the sand,

Beneath my feet.

Monster

We'll continue to live,

In a mind that confines us.

You and I both know,

That,

We all come undone.

All of this madness,

And all that surrounds us.

We'll continue to live,

In a mind that confines us,

If we continue to feed,

The monster inside us.

My First Child

I'll never forget,

Your first gaze, into my eyes,

The way it felt,

When they placed you in my arms.

Nothing else mattered,

The day I became your mother.

Although, I too

Was just a child, when you arrived,

I wouldn't change a thing,

Just to watch you smile.

Your the best part of me,

My first born child.

Landfall

Never will I, submit, to the destruction,

I feel within.

Raging like a hurricane,

As it creates chaos in the wind.

Ripping through the walls, of every

Part of my heart.

As the journey of this storm rages,

Landfall, makes its way,

And

When we think it's over,

It leaves destruction in its wake.

But, never will I, submit, to the destruction

I feel within,

It seems as though, my heart too,

Is raging, when landfall,

Makes its way through.

Never Meant To Stay

Hold me close, just one more time,

Before I let you go.

It aches my heart to walk away,

But in our hearts,

We both know,

We were never meant to stay.

Your soul speaks to me,

In ways, you'll never understand.

But in our hearts,

We both know,

We were never meant to stay.

So hold me close, just one more time.

Before I let you go.

Beauty And Bliss

All things made beautiful, from

Sunrise to nightfall.

The crisp fresh air, of rainfall.

Green trees, and ocean breeze,

The depths

Of the seven seas.

Pillow, cloud skies

Icebergs of heaven, move me,

I breathe in, the beauty of the earth,

All around me.

And though,

In this moment, I feel amiss,

I'll search for the embers,

Of beauty and bliss.

Unforetold Places

The heart can only take so much

Heartache,

Before it starts to crumble,

But, this strength,

Deep within me,

Will never allow me to stumble.

Let me, see the light,

In the unforetold places,

Where I search for pieces of

My soul, in the beauty of the

Darkest of spaces.

Illusion

It's getting hard to go on, when

I feel like I'm losing.

This nightmare inside me,

Feels like an illusion.

I feel an emptiness,

Down to my very core,

Impossible to ignore.

Calm the ache, inside my heart,

That cuts deep into,

The depths of my soul,

Where it once felt whole.

On The Surface

Lying to myself,

To feel okay on the surface,

Pushing down the pain in my chest,

I feel in this darkness.

God only knows, the weight,

I feel at this moment.

Lying to myself,

To feel okay on the surface.

Lead me, out of this darkness,

Where I can find my purpose.

Reflection

The reflection of the person,

I now see,

Isn't the girl I used to be.

The ghost in me,

Craves to see,

The reflection of the girl,

Known to me, so wild and free.

I don't crave perfection,

In my reflection,

Only to see the beauty, of the girl,

I used to be,

Looking back at me.

Mesmerize

I see it in the stars,

I see it in your eyes, mesmerized.

The light in your eyes,

That, brightens the dark,

Night skies.

A fire that cuts through,

The darkest of nights.

I see it in the stars,

I see it in your eyes, mesmerized,

A mesmerizing stillness,

Of fire,

Between your eyes and mine.

Compass

Lost in a world, without a compass.

You pull yourself, in every direction,

With no real destination.

Until the sun finds my face.

The energy of the sunsets evening breeze,

Blowing so effortless,

Between the trees.

The sail of the seven seas.

My heart aches for a tidal wave,

To bring me back to shore.

The undertow is treacherous, keeping me,

At the ocean floor.

Lost in a world without a compass,

Perhaps the sunsets everglades,

Can lead me back to the surface.